Community Learning & Libraries
Cymuned Ddysgu a Llyfrgelloedd

This item should be returned or renewed by the last date stamped below.

BLUE JOHN

BLUE JOHN

BERLIE DOHERTY

Illustrated by
Alexandria Neonakis

Barrington Stoke

First published in 2017 in Great Britain by
Barrington Stoke Ltd
18 Walker Street, Edinburgh, EH3 7LP

www.barringtonstoke.co.uk

Text © 2003 Berlie Doherty
Illustrations © 2017 Alexandria Neonakis

A CIP catalogue record for this book is available
from the British Library upon request

ISBN: 978-1-78112-578-6

Printed in China by Leo

This book is in a super readable format for young readers
beginning their independent reading journey.

*For Jane Nissen,
dear friend and editor*

CONTENTS

1 Ice 1

2 Fire 11

3 Song 23

4 Dance 35

5 Sun 49

6 Darkness 63

7 Heart 79

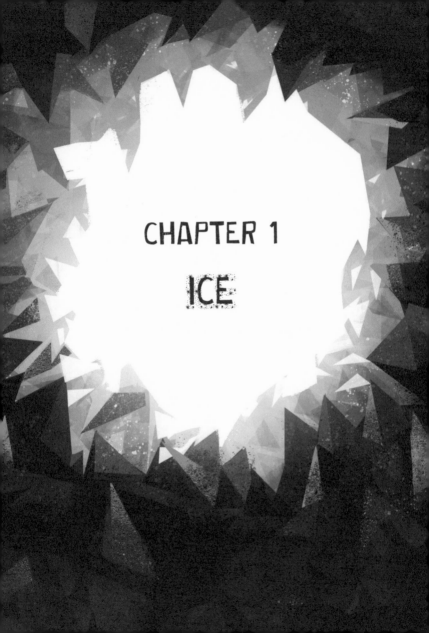

CHAPTER 1

ICE

Imagine a world that is locked in ice.
Imagine the purple-blue heart of a
glacier opening up to the gold of the sun.
The mountains of ice crack, and the gush
of rivers forces rocks apart.

Imagine the water surging into all
the hollows of the earth and billowing
down and down under the ground
to hollow out huge caves, massive
chambers of darkness.

That's where the Queen of Darkness lives. She lives for ever under the ground in the shadow of the mountain called Mam Tor. She loves the darkness, the velvet-cool, the long, long hush of silence. It is her home.

Before the thawing ice mountains rushed her downwards into the shelter of the cavern, the Queen of Darkness snatched two things that she could not bear to leave behind.

"I will take the purple-blue heart of the glacier," she sang, "because it is the most beautiful colour in the world. And I will take the gold of the sun."

She clasped the colours close to her as the waters swept her down into darkness, down and deep, deep down into the cavern that she was never to leave again.

"I don't know which of you I love the most," the Queen of Darkness crooned to her colours. "The blue of the glacier or the gold of the sun. Ice or fire. I love you both."

She pressed them to her, the one ice-cold and the other burning hot. She held them close and moulded them together like clay. Then she breathed on them and made a child, who was blue like the ice and gold like the sun.

"Blue John," she whispered. "Your name is Blue John, and you are mine for ever."

The Queen of Darkness kissed her child, and fell into a deep, deep sleep of enchantment that was to last for thousands of years.

CHAPTER 2

FIRE

Stalactites grew like coral, like twisted icicles, like the horns of unicorns, like the crooked teeth of goblins. Miners crept along the tunnels and chipped and hammered with their picks and tools. Their children crawled on hands and knees down the narrow passageways, holding candles in their mouths, pushing cartloads of lead and stone in front of them.

And still Blue John slept, and still the Queen of Darkness nursed him in her arms of rock.

And then, one day, Blue John woke up.

He gazed around him at the gleaming wet rocks and the drip, drip, dripping stalactites.

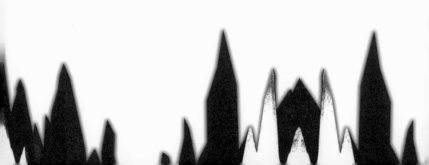

"Where am I?" he cried. "Oh, where am I? Where am I?"

Slowly Blue John stretched out his creaking limbs and climbed down from his high ledge. He rubbed his eyes and gazed around him. After a time he began to make out the shine of water on rocks and the high roof of the cavern over his head.

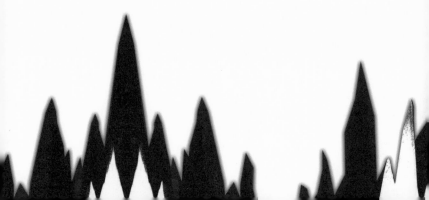

His feet slithered away from him and he toppled head over heels into a pool. He picked himself up and began again, skidding and sprawling, crawling and tumbling, and his footsteps chimed like bells.

"Who am I? Where am I? Oh, where am I? Am I? I? I?"

The Queen of Darkness laughed and put her strong, comforting arms around him.

"You're mine!" she whispered, like soft moss against his cheek. "You're

safe with me, Blue John! This is your home! But don't go into the light! You must never, never go into the light. You must stay here and make my dark cave beautiful. Now you can move around and dance and make it shine for me. But if you step outside and into the light, you will turn to stone and you will sleep for ever."

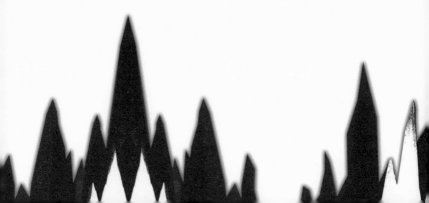

Blue John wandered down all the corridors and passages of the caverns. He wriggled through holes and slid down slides. He clambered into cracks and swung from stalactites. He splashed across pools and leaped from ledges.

And wherever he went the Queen of Darkness could see him, amethyst-blue and amber-gold, shining like ice and fire.

"Yes, Blue John," she sighed, "you are very beautiful. And you are mine!"

One day, as Blue John clambered up from the caves' deepest chambers, he heard sounds from outside.

He could hear, faint and far away, the call of the curlew on the moors, and the watery ripple of the skylark. He could hear the wind shimmying down the gorge of Winnats Pass and, far away, he could hear the bird-cries of children playing.

There was a tiny eye of light high up at the end of the passage. Blue John wanted to touch it. He felt drawn towards it as the sea is drawn by the moon. Yet he could hear the voice of his mother, pulling him back down to the safe darkness.

"Blue John! Blue John! Stay with me!"

But the sounds from outside were growing nearer. He could hear voices and footsteps, and the tiny high sound of someone singing. The sounds were coming towards the cavern. Dark shapes were blocking out the pinhole light of sky.

Blue John ran to the deepest chamber and hid there, afraid. "Who are they?" he cried. "Who are they?"

The Queen of Darkness laughed. "They're children!" she told him. "People come here to look at my caves, to wonder at my marvels and my mystery. Be still, and you can watch them. See how the creatures of light stumble and fall in my world. But never, never follow them into their world. Promise me, Blue John."

"I promise," he said.

Blue John clambered up onto his shelf and lay there, as still as stone. He watched and waited as the sounds of outside grew nearer, and he was a little bit excited, and he was a little bit afraid.

"And here they come," the Queen of Darkness said. "Here come the children!"

In they came, giggling and shouting and pushing each other.

Slipping and sliding and laughing out loud. Tripping and ducking and eating their sandwiches. Fumbling and falling and full of jokes and courage and sunshine.

But as they came further and deeper into the caverns, a hush grew over them.

Their voices sank down into whispers. They crept forward inch by inch, feeling with their soundless feet, blind as moles, hands clasping, and their breath was as quiet as ghosts around their lips.

They saw that the darkness was full of magic.

Blue John lay as still as the stones.
He had never seen children before. He
watched the wonder in their eyes. He
saw how their faces opened with awe
as his mother, the Queen of Darkness,
swirled silently around them.

One of the children struck a match. Its blue flame danced like a moth. Then the boy lit a candle and held it up so his face glowed like a moon and his eyes shimmered like stars. He passed the candle round and the other children lit theirs and held them up, and the cave was full of pale white moons and glittering stars. The lights of the candles flickered and gleamed on the wet walls.

A little girl with ribbons as green as trails of moss held out her candle towards Blue John's ledge.

There he was, lit up in the darkness, with his amethyst eyes purple and blue like the deepest glacier, and his amber hair as golden as the sun.

"Beautiful," the little girl whispered. "You're beautiful."

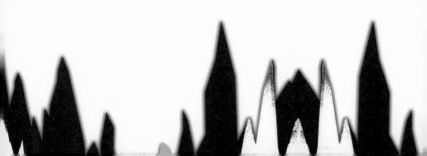

"You're beautiful," Blue John whispered back. "Beautiful."

The girl stepped into the middle of the chamber and began to move around, slowly, slowly. She held out her candle to light up the pockets and eyes and creases of the chamber, the satiny water on its walls, the shimmer and glisten, the blue and the gold. She began to dance.

And soon all the children were dancing in a crazy, laughing, happy way. Their shadows leaped around them.

Blue John tumbled down from his shelf and began to dance among them. He couldn't help himself. He flung out his arms and legs and he tossed back his head and his eyes were wide with happiness.

"Stop!" the Queen of Darkness screamed. "You're spoiling my silence. Stop dancing! Go away!"

She streamed around the children like the wind of night, and her cold breath chilled them and made their dance faster and wilder. She blew the candle flames so they flickered and flattened like birds.

"Go away!"

And the children ran, dancing and laughing. They tumbled out of the Queen's chamber and up along the echoing passages, dancing and laughing, singing and skipping, out into the brilliant light of day.

And then they were gone.

As fast as they had come, the children had disappeared, and their voices and laughter and the sunshine of the outside world had gone with them.

CHAPTER 5

SUN

Blue John was alone with the silence. He searched among the shadows of the caverns, he listened to the darkness, but there was no trace left of the children or of the little smiling girl with ribbons of moss in her hair who had danced for him.

Blue John crept up the long corridor that led to the mouth of the caves and stood looking out. He didn't know it was possible to feel such sadness.

"Where are you, little smiling girl?" he whispered. His whisper spun away from him and echoed back down the chamber to the Queen of Darkness.

"Where are you? Where are you?"

He crept as far as he dared towards the eye-light of day. It burned his eyes, yet still he peered out.

"Where are you?"

Far below, Blue John could see the children running down the green slopes towards the village. His smiling girl was at the back. Almost as if she knew he was there watching her, she stopped and turned. She looked back up the hill and she lifted her hand, just as if she was waving to him.

Blue John lifted his hand, just a little.

"Blue John, I made you out of ice and fire," the Queen of Darkness whispered, and her voice echoed and sighed around the twisting passages. "I made you for myself, to make my darkness beautiful."

Blue John felt as if his heart was going to break in two.

"Stay with me," the Queen of Darkness said. "You can only live in the shadows."

"I know," said Blue John. "I know."

But he turned away from his Queen
and stepped out into the sunshine, into
the brilliant golden day.

The Queen of Darkness was wild with anger and sorrow, with jealousy and grief.

She swirled like a whirlwind around her caves and grottos, crying out for Blue John to come home. Her breath was black and cold as nightmares, and her eyes were glittering ebony. Her walls and rivers streamed.

"Come home!" the Queen of Darkness cried. "You can't live in the world of light! You belong to the darkness for ever!"

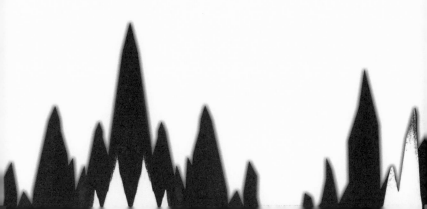

CHAPTER 6

DARKNESS

The children were playing in the school playground. They shouted and laughed to one another about how their candles had blown out in the cavern just like that, and how they had turned and stumbled along the tunnels of darkness, clinging to one another.

"You were scared!" one shouted.

"No I wasn't! You were!" another shouted back.

And they tossed the fun of being afraid backwards and forwards like a bouncing ball.

But deep inside themselves they held the quiet magic of the caverns. That was a secret, never to be forgotten.

The little girl with green ribbons sat on her own, long after the other children had run back home.

She thought about Blue John, and how he had shone in the darkness, and how he had danced with her, just her.

And when she looked up, there he was, running down the grassy slant of the mountain.

"Blue John!" she called. "I'm here!"

He raced towards her, hopping and skipping and tumbling head over heels over the bracken and the heather, laughing out loud.

She caught his hands in hers and they danced. They swung each other round until it seemed as if the birds and the clouds and the trees and the rocky green bones of the mountain were spinning round over their heads, and they would never stop spinning, never.

But the Queen of Darkness called to him.

"Come home, Blue John. Come home!"

Her voice rose out of the rocks and the earth.

The sides of the mountain heaved with her voice. Its deep shadow fell across the valley. The light of the sun drained from the sky and the blue slipped away to grey. Blue John could feel his blood slowing down and his limbs growing heavy as stones.

He dropped his hands away from the girl's. He turned away from her. He could hardly walk. He climbed slowly back to the cavern and crept to the deep chamber where he lived. He clambered onto his ledge and stretched himself out, with the weariness of thousands of years closing down on him. He couldn't keep his eyes open.

The Queen of Darkness bent over
him and hummed a song that was like
the murmur of ice stretching in sunlight.
She rocked him in her quiet arms. Soon
the deep sleep of her enchantment
washed over him. His eyes closed, and
the purple-blue of their colour seeped
into the stones. The golden yellow of
his hair poured like the light of the sun
down the walls of the cavern.

Crystals of ice and fire gleamed in
the darkness.

CHAPTER 7

HEART

The girl with ribbons like trailing moss in her hair came into the cavern alone. She walked down the long dripping passages and across the hollow chambers until she came to the deepest chamber of all.

"Where are you?" she called, and her own voice answered her. "Where are you? Where are you? Where are you?"

Lying on the ground was a shining piece of rock. It was blue and yellow. The girl picked it up, and closed her hand around it. And, did she imagine this? Could she feel it beating, like a tiny heart?

"Take it," the dark echoes whispered to her, and whispered again down all the corridors.

"Take it. Keep it safe. It's for you."